HASLEY

FATELESS

For Emilia S. Morrow.
Together, we break down walls.

THE
FATED TALES

HASLEY

FATELESS

ONLY LOVE CAN HEAL
THE ECHOING MADNESS.

R. K. SAMPSON

unavoidable and magically-induced love at first sight

- Depictions of a magically-induced mental illness and harm coming to people with this illness
- Discussion of the death of a spouse and mother and dealing with grief
- Discussions from an LGBTQ+ character where they aren't sure how they fit into a system

There is a fire tunneling through my heart.

Run, it says.

Run, don't look back.

I don't know if I can. I don't know if I can run fast enough or far enough to escape it. It burns through each beat, beat, beat, like the sound of feet on pavement.

I'm worried it will reach my soul soon. That it'll rip me open if I don't obey.

Run, it says, *to the wall.*

PART 1
BEFORE

ONE

CARRIAGES

An anger that was unlike Hasley's usual disposition boiled in her veins. How could Ember do this to her? They were best friends. In fact, Hasley was Ember's only friend. Didn't that mean they should tell each other everything? Hasley's heart hammered in her chest as she walked into the back of the jewelry shop Ember and her apprenticed at.

Her fingers gripped the paper in her hands, crumbling the edges as she stared at her friend's empty workbench. When Hasley had come into purpose apprenticeship that morning, her only care had been to ask Amlin Jeweler, her mentor, if he had heard from Ember. After Ember didn't come back from her delivery the day before, Hasley had begun to fear the worst. She walked back to Ember's home and found that Ember hadn't returned there either. If Amlin hadn't heard anything, Hasley's next stop would be to report her absence to the province guards. What if one of the Fateless had hurt her?

It happened sometimes. Those crippled by the madness were prone to acting out in violence. This was one of the reasons why the Fateless were often *silenced* by the province guards. The Fateless were too dangerous to be allowed to live, and while Hasley found that difficult to stomach, she understood it.

That is, she did until recently. But she pushed that thought aside. This morning she was angry, not sad and confused. She was not going to focus on her own concerns when her best friend was revealed to be the missing princess.

The dragon daughter had been missing for sixteen years, stolen from the newly minted dragon queen's birthing bed. Despite the many years that have passed, Karwyn Dragon Queen and her consort, Jedoriah Knight, were not blessed with another heir to Ashkadance's throne.

Hasley hadn't thought too much about it, unlike other citizens. She instead focused on her future, rather than that of the crown. Their god Mutrien and goddess Aaleia would not leave the throne without a ruler, she had reasoned, so she didn't need to worry.

And apparently, she was right. Ember was the heir. Her best friend was a princess in hiding and Hasley didn't know.

Hasley wanted to kick herself. She had been worried all night, thinking something terrible must have befallen her friend. Instead, notices were passed out at dawn and pasted on every building to spread the happy news. The princess was found, alive, and had been in Firetop under the name Ember Julimore.

How could she not have told her?

The crumbled notice fell to the floor.

Amlin Jeweler walked into the back room, the door slamming behind him. Wherever he went, he made plenty of noise. His default was a shuffling walk that spoke of disinterest. Today he walked faster, his intent leaving loud and purposeful steps.

"Did you know this?" he asked Hasley in an accusational tone, as if she were tainted by a secret she didn't know. His yellow eyes squinted and his skin appeared burnt from recent sun exposure.

"I-I..." Hasley struggled to find the words.

Her anger simmered and she instead felt drowned in dread. How did Ember's true identity impact her purpose apprenticeship here? Amlin controlled whether or not she would receive her purpose name as a jeweler. She had been working towards this for a year and it could all tumble down.

Nothing was going according to plan. She would get an apprenticeship, get her purpose name, move out, get fated, and open her own shop with Ember. Ember would do all the actual jewelry-making, as Hasley always knew. But with this big mysterious moment before her, Hasley realized without Ember's talent, was she anything at all?

Why did Ember keep this from her? Her hurt bubbled to the surface. She wasn't truly angry, Hasley knew. She was heartbroken and mourning a future she thought they had together as friends.

Hasley ran from the confrontation, making her way passed the market and to the inns. Bounding down the street, she felt her feet hit stone as if it were her heart. She hastily pulled up her blue hair as it whipped around her. If Ember was still here, as the other workers on the street had been gossiping this morning, maybe she could fix this, somehow.

"I don't know. I don't understand," Hasley muttered to herself as she ran, answering unvoiced questions.

When she reached the inns, she saw there were dozens of people already gathered at the end of the street. She could only get five people deep, pushing between them to see guards in purple holding everyone back. The street was blocked off and she pleaded with them to let her through. Grumbles came from behind her over her rude interruption of their own gawking.

Were they ever friends? Why was she hiding for so long? Did Ember not trust Hasley?

She wasn't who she thought. She was the royal heir. And Hasley had no idea. Hasley wasn't trusted. Hasley was alone. How could she compare to the future Queen?

*To the wall...*a voice whispered in her mind.

"Not now!" Hasley screamed and the guard she had been pleading with a moment prior looked to her annoyed.

Over the guard's shoulder, the street was clear save for two anchoris pulled carriages. Figures far away walked towards them. Hasley lost her breath as she recognized one of the figures as Ember, unmistakable with her black hair reflecting the sheen of a rainbow in the sunlight.

"Ember!" Hasley screamed, desperate to break from the crowd.

Her best friend did not turn around. Instead, she entered the carriage without a second glance. As the carriages rolled away, Hasley fell to the floor in a heap. She wanted to cry and admit she was alone, letting her self-pity take over. But on the floor, she saw an opening and crawled around the guard's feet. Hasley pumped her legs as hard as she could down the street, two guards hot on her heels, but she was too late.

The carriages were already further than she could reach. Hasley stopped running and took one long sobbing breath. The future she thought she had with her best friend rolled away in an elegantly drawn carriage.

TWO

ROCKS IN REALITY

ELEVEN YEARS AGO

"I love going to school, Momma," Hasley said with a smile. She skipped between her and her dad, holding their hands and swinging them back and forth.

"That's wonderful, little darling," Hasley's mom, Mayree said.

"What's your favorite part about it?" her father, Clove, asked.

"I love having a friend. Ember is silly, but I like her," Hasley replied. Ember didn't speak much, but Hasley didn't mind. It was easy for Hasley to talk and for Ember to listen.

They were only a couple of buildings away from the school. They walked together every day before Mayree and Clove would attend to their purposes.

Hasley's only priority, until she was fifteen, was schooling. After that, she would work as an apprentice until she was deemed ready to take on her purpose. Many people were able to get to purpose within two or three years, but sometimes it could take up to five. It wasn't uncommon to try two different apprenticeships, just to be sure.

When she was ready, Hasley Mayree would become someone new. Her purpose would overtake her mother's name, and Hasley would take on a new purpose identity.

Hasley didn't like to think of that future, not yet anyway. She had eleven years to think about it. Thinking about romance was much more exciting. Even though, admittedly, it would likely take just as long to find her fated pair.

"Why do you say that?" her mom asked curiously. They stood at the gates of her school and Mayree kneeled before her to adjust Hasley's braided hair.

"She likes rocks and shiny things, it's silly."

"Oh, I love shiny things! I must be silly too," her father teased.

"Dad, no, you can't be silly. Moms and Dads aren't silly," Hasley said and shook her head. Adjusting her bag on her shoulder, she turned and walked into the school. Her parents called a goodbye behind her and went on their way.

Sitting in her assigned seat, she bounced up and down waiting for Ember to walk through the door and sit beside her. In her pocket was a present for her friend, a smooth stone she found near the wall on the way home. It was different from other rocks she'd seen, especially with its thin and almost perfectly circular shape. Hasley couldn't wait to give it to her.

As time passed and the teacher began to speak, Hasley frowned and surveyed the desks again. Ember hadn't sat in a different seat, where was she? When the time for their scheduled break came, Hasley walked up to the teacher. Other students walked around her and out to their activities.

"Is Ember sick today?" Hasley asked.

"No Hasley. Ember's mothers withdrew her from school yesterday. She moved to another province," Hasley's teacher said. She pulled out some papers from her desk with a dismissive hand wave. She remained unaware of the impact her statement held on the five-year-old.

Hasley turned away, walking to the playground where the other kids laughed and played together.

"She didn't say goodbye," Hasley said to no one as her little hand gripped the stone to her heart.

THREE

Hasley didn't go to her purpose apprenticeship the next day or the day after. She stayed home, feeling like her life slip away as the splinter in her mind grew. A letter arrived from Ember on the fourth day.

Hasley,

It is with shaking hands that I write this to you. First of all, I am so sorry that I never made it back to the shop that day. I can imagine how scary that must have been when I did not return. I am sorry to have done that to you, as I know what it is like to wait for someone that doesn't come back. If I could have changed it, I would have. I even tried escaping by setting an inn on fire. It wasn't one of

my proudest moments. In fact, it was an embar-
rassing failure. But not long after, I learned the
truth.

Ever since I was born, I had scales on my
chest. My moms told me it was dangerous to
talk about or reveal and that we needed to keep
a low profile. I was the reason we moved so
frequently, so they could shelter me. But now
I'm told they were my kidnappers, not my
blessed parents by birth, and I feel so much
conflict in my heart. They say that my blessed
parents were actually Karwyn Dragon Queen
and Jedoriah Knight. Based on what has
happened so far, I believe them. That belief
hurts.

I love my moms and despite the fear they
instilled in me over being different...I miss them. I
wish they were experiencing this with me and
helping to guide me. I'm so lost right now, Hasley.
My moms are dead and can't answer my questions. I have so many. I am so confused.

I kept so much from you. You were my only
friend, Hasley, in all these years. I felt so guilty
not confiding in you. Will you forgive me? I did
not know I was a princess, but I did know I was
different. It would have been better to have

*confided in you, but after my moms died I was so
scared that my secrets would kill you too.*

With love,
Ember

Hasley wasn't sure if that made it worse or better. Ember had still kept something monumental from her —scales. Even if she didn't know about being a princess, Hasley could have helped carry that burden.

But the worst thing of all was the fact that Hasley hadn't thought of Ember's feelings at all. She assumed this was somehow what she wanted, that she had left to be a princess. As if she had known all along this was her future, and hadn't intended to run a shop with Hasley. Hasley had never felt more inferior and alone. There was only so much blame Hasley could throw on Ember because Hasley too was keeping a secret.

Ember always kept quiet and attempted to be unnoticeable. Hasley had been Ember's only friend, but Hasley herself had many friends over the years. But friends were often a distraction. She had let them all go, except for Ember.

And now knowing who, and what, she was...it didn't make the jealousy she felt for her friend any better. Hasley hated her jealousy, wished she could stamp out the ill feelings of unworthiness she felt daily, but she didn't know how.

One day later, Hasley's mom knocked and came into her room. "Good morning," she said.

Hasley pulled the covers away from her face at the sound of her mother's voice.

Mayree's smile was comforting as she handed over two notes. "These were left outside our door, dear. Can I help you get up and ready for your purpose?"

Hasley read over the first note, recognizing the handwriting.

If you come back, you will get your purpose name.

At least one thing went according to plan. Or, did it? Would she have received the jeweler name if Ember hadn't left?

Hasley's mother brought her clean clothes and a comb. She accepted it as gracefully as she could despite the hazy feelings and disorientation of her mind. Her mom had chosen for her the yellow dress she had worn the year before to the first day of her apprenticeship. She was closing the door on who she used to be, in more ways than one.

Hasley pulled her hair into a messy bun and

walked from her room to go to her purpose. She pushed outside the door, realizing that when she walked in she would no longer be Hasley Mayree. She would be Hasley Jeweler. She had always wanted that, why hesitate now?

She walked into the jewelry shop with the second letter still unfurled in her pocket. She knew it was from Ember, her mother had read it and said so. Yet she felt the need to shield herself from more words until she was at another location, for fear she would scare her family further.

The second letter from Ember was as short as Amlin's, likely scribbled only hours after the first one and sent with speed. She opened the letter beside her counter in Amlin's shop while a customer peered into a case nearby.

My debut bull is in two weeks. Will you come as my guest?

To the wall, the whisper told her, interrupting her thoughts with one she didn't choose.

"Shut up," Hasley said aloud, shaking her head.

"I didn't say anything," the customer said, eyebrows raised.

"Sorry," Hasley apologized before going back to

rearranging the files behind the counter. "Don't embarrass me," she whispered to herself. The bell above the door rang as the customer left.

To the wall, the voice said again.

Amlin walked into the front room with a few boxes of finished jewelry. "Can you unpack these?" he asks her and wipes his mouth. She busied herself with the task, noticing a stain on the corner of the larger one as she put the jewelry into the display cases. She opens it to find a lemon pie, one piece missing.

She looked up at him, expecting Amlin to realize his mistake and take back the pie to the workroom.

"Uh," he stammered, "happy purpose name day. I got you a pie, but then I wasn't sure if you'd come back, so I ate a piece...it's good."

"Thank you," Hasley said in astonishment, not used to Amlin being thoughtful.

He coughed and shuffled his feet. "Yeah, anyway, I sent your papers to the local Keyholder's office. You're officially a jeweler..." he trailed off and nodded.

Hasley swallowed hard, feeling the need to isolate herself as Ember must have. She can't go to see her now. If she went to the castle and was recognized as fateless, then Ember herself may have to give the order to kill her. She shook her head again, pushing away the images flashing before her eyes. She shouldn't have come back here, purpose name or not.

"Right, okay, well tomorrow you are on delivery duty. We're closing early today, too many nosy neighbors asking after *her* and not buying anything," Amlin said without naming Ember.

Hasley nodded, unsure if she could speak.

In another unexpected moment of sincerity, Amlin put a hand on her shoulder and said, "We'll be okay without her, we'll survive."

She attempted a smile, but she knew it did not meet her eyes.

FOUR

TO THE WALL

That night, Hasley's pupils grew large as the walls of her bedroom seemed to flicker in and out of existence. Her eyes attempted to take in more light and detail to reorient where she was. It was a fruitless effort. Hasley was falling victim to the plague that had harmed many of their citizens and she could no longer hide it.

"I'm in my room, I'm in my room, I'm in my room," she repeated. She hugged her knees closer and grounded her feet down on top of her sheets. There was fabric between her toes and cushion under her butt. She was in her bed. Hasley thought on what she touched, smelled, and heard. They all matched what she would expect of her bedroom. But what she saw did not meet her reality.

The walls of her bedroom flickered in front of her. In the moments between, she saw the peiradoone wall of the kingdom. It was difficult to see in the dark, but she would know that wall anywhere.

Go, go, go to the wall.

"No. I'm in my room. I'm staying in my room," she said. Hasley squeezed her eyes shut, hoping to see nothing but the inside of her eyelids. Instead, stars were visible.

"No no no no no no no," Hasley whimpered. She dropped her knees, threw the blanket over her, and curled into a ball.

"My name is Hasley Jeweler. I am the daughter of Mayree and Clove. I live in Firetop. I am friends with Ember Juli—Ember Dragon Daughter. I was an apprentice, now I have my purpose. I am saving for a house of my own. Soon I will be fated."

Hasley's voice tripped on the last whispered sentence, letting her fear of what was happening to her seep in.

"Soon I will be fated. I am not fateless. I am not fateless. I am Hasley Jeweler."

Hasley whispered into the night, rocking back and forth until her mom found her. By morning, Hasley's eyes were glazed and pointed towards the wall of her bedroom. Her face was stained with tears. Her mother walked into the room and out again with a hand over her mouth. She was back a moment later with her pair beside her.

Hasley could no longer deny what was happening. She had to decide what to do now, before her parents had to choose for her.

Hasley's parents helped her out of bed and into the bathroom. Her mom helped her into the bath as her dad brought in a fresh towel. Hasley blinked away her thoughts and asked them to leave while she finished up. They sighed, as if her words took away all worries momentarily. Her parents closed the door behind them with a click. Hasley got out of the tub a few minutes later and put back on the yellow dress she had slept in. She didn't have spare clothes in the bathroom. She focused on the mirror above the sink and cringed at the circles under her eyes. With regret, Hasley walked back to her room to gather her things. It was time.

She paused every few steps, taking in the sights of their ancestral home. In the hallway, she would lay out her dolls and hold shows as a child. In the storage room at the end of the hall, she would play hide and seek. The living room, a short distance from her bedroom, where she would spend time telling stories with her parents by the fire.

Her room no longer looked like the wall surrounding Ashkadance. Instead of the pain and disorder from the night before, the peach walls and sunlight through the window brought out her inner calm. She surveyed the room and picked up a small bag. She stuffed it quickly with a few basic clothing items and momentos. On her way out she opened up her jewelry box and picked up the small smooth stone she kept there. She tried not to think of what she was leaving behind in her quick packing.

This wouldn't be her home anymore. The future she imagined for her life was no more. Her parents looked up from the kitchen and halted their whispered conversation as they heard her steps. She didn't say goodbye, she knew her voice would not remain even if she did.

Hasley, heartbroken, walked out the door without a word. Who knew if their paths would ever cross again.

Hasley pulled a slip of paper from her bag and handed it to the neighborhood wraith as she passed.

Amlin won't let me go to the ball. I'm sorry.
-Hasley

The lie came easier than she would like. Hasley

knew she could not see Ember or anyone from the royal family this way, not when the Fateless were typically killed on sight.

Hasley turned left to Mount Pietan instead of the most direct route to her purpose. She walked silently up the steps she had run down just a few days before. Today, she didn't care that it was past the morning mountain curfew. It wasn't like she could attend to her purpose now anyway.

Find the docks, the voice said.

Hasley stopped walking. There were no docks, what could the voice mean?

Men and women walked into the entrances to the mine below her. Mount Pietan, while also the religious site of the First Fating, was where Ashkadance sourced their largest resource—peiradoone stone. Every structure in the kingdom was made from it. It was a mostly fire-proof substance.

That was more helpful in prior generations, when there were dragons. Minors worked within the mountain during her purpose hours. Visitors were only allowed up to the First Fating statue at dawn and dusk.

No one knew where the full-sized dragons were now, but Hasley was used to seeing some of their demi-breeds. The wraiths that delivered letters and the anchoris who worked to draw carriages long distances were both a type of dragon.

Reaching her destination, Hasley looked up at the statues of the first and only dragon king, Drakul, and the first of a line of dragon queens, Karianna. She bent to her knees before them and prayed, not caring about the dirt and grass staining her knees.

"You shouldn't be here!" the older woman said. Her long pink hair was now streaked more grey than pink, bringing out her sallow complexion. It was the same reaction she had told Ember the last time they were here. Hasley knew she would come.

"I know," Hasley called out. "I need to speak with you."

Whether it was the fact that Hasley had knelt on the ground or the general dismay on her face that convinced the priestess that she could stay—Hasley was unsure. The priestess motioned with an outstretched hand to the cluster of buildings off in the distance. They seemed older than other buildings in the province, their peiradoone stone more grey than white. Hasley stood and they walked beside each other in silence for several long minutes. Hasley glanced at the priestesses robes from the side of her eye. She wondered how often there were visitors to the priestesses.

"What brings you here?" she asked with a casual air. The priestesses all spoke in a level tone, almost monotonous. Other than when they were yelling at you about the mountain curfew, that is. It depended on Hasley's mood on whether or not she believed they sounded wise or creepy.

"I need guidance," Hasley said, turning her eyes back to the grass and her feet.

"Guidance on what?" the priestess prodded.

"I fear..." Hasley hesitated and they both stopped walking. They were a short distance from their destination.

"I fear that I am becoming fateless," Hasley whispered. Her body shuddered at the word.

The woman wrapped an arm around Hasley's shoulder with a tight smile and they resumed walking.

"You came to the right place."

A NEW PURPOSE

The inside of the compound was one surprise after the other. Despite having only seen the pink-haired priestess on the mountain, there seemed to be dozens of priestesses. Like all buildings in Ashkadance, this one was built out of peiradoone stone.

On the inside, there were dozens of shelves of books in many shapes and sizes. There were several doors and hallways visible from the main room, but Hasley was ushered into the second room to the right. The carpet beneath the room's long desk was a warm red. A stack of papers, pens, and other small items left haphazardly on one side, with the other half of the desk clean. It was as if whoever worked here gave up reorganizing half-way through the task. The priestess left Hasley alone for a moment in the small office before coming back in with a man also dressed in robes. What was he doing here? Hasley had thought only priestesses looked after the statue of the First Fating and the priests maintained the cathedral in Mutrien.

They bid her to share how she came to be there. After keeping her fears close to her chest for weeks, the details spilled easily from Hasley's mouth. She told them about the voice inside her, the change in her emotions and the outbursts, as well as the disturbances in her vision from the night before.

"You have a purpose, Hasley Fateless," the pink priestess said. Her companion with black hair and pale skin nodded.

"Don't call me that," Hasley snapped. She shook in her seat, too cold in the room the priestess led her to. The bottom of the chair bit into her bare legs, the yellow dress too flimsy a covering.

She quieted, regretting her quick reaction. "I'm sorry, I didn't mean to yell. But please, don't call me that. My purpose name is Jeweler."

The priestess gave a sympathetic nod before speaking again.

"I'm sorry to say that it is not. Given what you have described to us, you are indeed one of the Fateless. Being fateless is your new path. We don't have all the answers, but we have some for you." She gestured to the man beside her.

"What kind of answers?" Hasley asked hopefully. "Do you know how to fix me?" Hasley looked between the two, needing a sliver of hope she could cling too.

"We can't fix you, because you are not broken."

Hasley disagreed and the silver lining she had hoped for withered as quickly as it bloomed.

"We have worked with many of the Fateless. Many stay here with us, others have joined the resistance, some we never see again. But there is one thing in common, those that have the voices are often the most lucid. They are asked to find people, to go places, or they have a task. We believe it is a mission from the gods."

Hasley looked between the man and woman before her, wondering if she truly was mad or if they were.

"How do you know?"

"These voices have led to secret missions in the resistance, with Keyholders, and with Scribemaster. It has brought us closer to the goal of dismantling the wall. And those that listen to the voice and help them, seem to be more lucid or more like themselves after."

Hasley was shocked to hear them speak so openly

of going against the royal family. Shouldn't the priestesses be loyal to the family chosen by their god and goddess? Being against the wall wasn't a shock on it's own. It was something often whispered between friends. Yet, talking openly about working to dismantle it? That made Hasley's heart beat faster than it already was. Is this the group she would put her trust in? But Hasley would do much to feel normal again, to find her pair. Maybe even go against the family that now included her best friend.

"So after they complete their mission, the people with voices feel okay?" Hasley asked hopefully, latching on too feeling more normal.

"Fatelessness isn't a disease, so there isn't a cure. It is a byproduct of speaking to the gods. Only the beasts, or those that are part beast, like the Drakul line, can fully hear and interpret the message without as much harm to the mind. Prolonged communication, that might still impact them, but us humans feel the effect immediately," said the man. He listed off each sentence as an irrefutable fact, tapping them off on the table.

"Well, that's one interpretation," the woman interjected, "Those labeled as part of the Fateless are not pairless. They simply cannot get to them because of the wall or another reason. Not all of the Fateless hear voices, so I find this most likely." She nodded and patted the man's hand before continuing, "there are likely fateless in the other kingdoms, the pairs that should have met our people."

"We agree to disagree," he replied. "But in either case, we can't learn more while the wall is in place."

Hasley felt dejected. Her emotions changed rapidly with each small piece of information. The fact that none of it may be true added to her despair. Hasley realized they were all playing a dangerous guessing game. How could any of these theories be tested? Would she ever be normal again? Tears welled in her eyes.

"Maybe I'm cursed," Hasley whispered. "I was never good enough. Not worthy. A horrible and jealous friend with simple aspirations and no genuine contribution to the world. The gods want to be rid of me."

"No, no, Hasley," the woman said. "You are not cursed. None of the Fateless are, no matter what some people say. Aaleia and Mutrien are helping us, we just don't see how yet. Nothing you have done or didn't do made you deserve this. For all we know, the answer to it all lies in you, Hasley."

She walked out from behind the desk and leaned beside Hasley's chair.

"Trust this was for a reason, something happening for you and not to you. When this is over, Hasley, you'll be able to tell us what that reason was. For now, would you like a place to stay while you decide what to do?"

Hasley nodded mutely as the tears rolled down her face.

"Good, you are welcome with us," the priestess said, "until you find out what you would like to do. Whether that be wait, or take action." She shook her head and rolled her eyes, realizing something.

"I didn't introduce myself. I apologize. I am Flair," the pink-haired woman said. "And this is my pair, Boyrn. We run this compound together."

"It's nice to meet you both," Hasley said with a tremor, "thank you for taking me in."

"You aren't alone, Hasley. We have other fateless here who have taken refuge with us. Many have felt the called to come here, near the First Fating," Boyrn said. He stood and together he and Flair showed Hasley where she would be sleeping.

HIDDEN MISSIONS

Hasley hadn't spoken to her family in over a week. She hoped her mother and father were okay, letting herself linger on them more than she had the past few days. At least, Hasley reasoned, this may be easier for them. With her disappearance, they wouldn't have to choose whether or not to turn her in. That guilt would be a lot to bear, Hasley reasoned. Hopefully, not knowing was easier.

The voice's tone was no longer as harried or fearful. It seemed to calm while living on the top of Mount Pietan, and for a while, Hasley avoided making a decision. Which, in essence, was a choice to stay and feel the calm a little while longer. She'd wake up and say "not today" to anything the voice requested and would sleep away as much of the day as she could.

There weren't any more blurred and shattered visions. Her eyes unwaveringly displayed what was before her. For now, the forest did not forcibly replace her sight.

Tonight felt different. The voice murmured to her *listen, listen, listen,* and she felt that was a harmless enough request.

Hasley sat cross-legged on her cot, watching the other occupants of the hidden living quarters.

She surveyed the state of all the fateless that the priest and priestesses have taken in. What were their stories? Did they try to take the burden from their family too? Or were they abandoned and found their way here?

The room held lines of cots full of people just like her. The majority of the people there were near Hasley's age or slightly older. Some were sitting, like Hasley, or reading and writing. Others stared blankly up at the ceiling. A few in the bunch were strapped to their bed and thrashing, Hasley tried not to look at them for too long. Those thrashing fateless laid bunched together towards one end of the room, isolated from the rest. It hurt to know that she could become like them. Priestesses moved between those that could not help themselves, providing water and food.

"Here he is," Flair said.

Hasley turned to the voice. Flair and Boyrn were leading an older man into the room. One of the men on a cot nearby stood. Hasley was close enough to hear their voices among the crowd.

"It's a pleasure to meet you, Amic Keyholder, I am James," the fateless man said and shook the stranger's hand.

"A pleasure. I hear you have a message for me," Amic replied.

A keyholder? Wouldn't it be dangerous to have someone that ran one of Ashkadance's provinces, and likely knew the royal family, here? What would Ember think if she found out Hasley was here?

Go to him, the voice whispered. Hasley felt a warmness spread in her chest in response. She stood without thought and walked to where they spoke.

"And I'm Hasley," she said and inserted herself to the conversation. She looked in Amic's brown eyes and felt something snap into place in her reality. *Follow him. He needs you.*

Unbidden, she said, "I'll be leaving with you."

A second later she came back to reality, embarrassed to have spoken out of turn to someone she didn't know. This was not how things were done.

"Oh really?" he said with a quirked eyebrow.

"Hasley receives messages as well," Boyrn interjected.

James looked to her and Amic. "Looks like you are a popular Keyholder," he said.

"There is plenty of me to go around," Amic joked. "Let's start by going somewhere more private."

Boyn led them back to the office Hasley was in the week before. Once inside, they walked through a back door she hadn't noticed before. Inside appeared to be a scribe shop. There are books everywhere, like a library and their outer halls, but with stations open with empty pages ready to be transcribed. One woman was steadily at work, but at the nod of Boyrn she existed from the door they walked through.

"You won't be overheard in here," Boyrn assured them and exited.

The thick door closed behind him with a resounding thud.

Amic sat in one of the chairs along the long center table. He gestured to the opposite chairs and Hasley and James sat down, wryly glancing at each other.

"Mind if I go first?" James asked Hasley. She nodded at him, not sure at all what she'll say next. She asked the voice in her mind why she was here, but it didn't answer.

"I saw you in my dreams," the boy began, "you

were underground, with barrels engulfed in flame. When I woke up..." he hesitated.

"Yes, James?" Amic prodded, wrapped in what he was saying.

"That's when the voice started speaking to me. It said I needed to find you."

"Did it call me by name specifically?"

"Yes," James said.

Hasley felt jealous for a moment. Why was the voice so clear with him? Maybe she was the regular old fateless, someone going mad, while this boy got the real messages from the gods?

"Did you see what happened after the barrels caught fire?" His eyes were intent on James, focused.

"No, I only saw you in the room as it was filled with smoke."

"Why does the voice want you to find me?"

"I don't know, but I assume it's because I do well with special compounds. If it can be combined to make something or is flammable, I have a knack for studying and caring for it. It's gotten me in a lot of trouble at times. But if you are doing something with fire, maybe I can help for once."

Amic studied the boy, searching his face for something unknown to them before he nodded.

"Alright, want to come with me to Borderain to see what I'm working on?"

"Yes, very much so, Amic Keyholder," James sighed in relief, as if his job were half done.

"You've got it. We leave in the morning."

He shifted his searching gaze to Hasley, "now why do you want to come with me?"

Amic folded his hands together on the table.

"I don't know," she said honestly. "I don't have a very clear voice. Maybe I'm just broken," Hasley said with a wet laugh.

Amic shook his head in disagreement.

"Just because you don't know why you are here, doesn't mean you weren't meant to be here."

He stood and walked around the perimeter of the room, idly trailing a finger along the spines of books.

"What were you doing before you found yourself here, Hasley?" he asked as his finger grazed the spines of the books he passed, seemingly more curious of his surroundings than her. The blue of his shirt stood out brightly in the room, probably just as much as her own blue hair did wherever she went.

"I was a jeweler," she said. At least, she was an official jeweler for one day. She'd keep that detail to herself.

He turned his head slightly, but continued to walk

around the room as if their conversation was more casual than it really was. "Did you know Amlin Jeweler?"

"I worked for him," Hasley whispered, guessing where his thoughts were leaning towards.

Amic paused, his hand gripping the book his finger happened to be on. "You knew the princess," he said.

"I did—I do," Hasley amended.

Amic turned around and held his hands wide to the two seated fateless teens.

"I think we'll make a good team. I have a lot to show you both."

His smile spoke of promises and secrets, Hasley was not reassured.

SEVEN

THE OCEAN

The days that followed held bumpy roads, but warm beds. The province of Borderain was only a few days away from Firetop, where Hasley and Ember had resided. Hasley traveled with Amic and James in silence for the first two days. Amic did not give many details about what he was working on, suggesting that they had to see it for themselves. A few weeks ago that would have bothered Hasley, but at this moment there was more on her mind.

When they were only a few hours from his province, he began to inquire deeper about their lives. Most of all, he asked Hasley about her time with Ember.

"Did you know she was the dragon daughter?" Amic asked as they rode in the carriage.

There was enough space for Hasley, James, and Amic to sit comfortably across the two benches. Hasley sat on one side to herself, leaning against the window.

"No, I didn't," Hasley answered. She wished she could have helped her friend carry that secret, but Ember didn't give her that opportunity.

"How long have you known each other?" Unlike the first leg of the journey, Amic and James watched her instead of the changing scenery outside the carriage windows.

"For a year in elementary education, then just this past year."

"Why not in between?" Amic asked. Hasley asked herself that same question when her friend had came back after all those years.

"She moved away. Her moms didn't stay in one province for too long. I'm sure they've lived in your province too."

He paused at that, the thought hadn't crossed his mind prior.

"Did she make any other friends during these moves?"

"No, just me." Hasley didn't know that for sure,

but Ember never brought up other people, or sent letters to friends she met along the way. She only ever spoke about her moms, or Hasley herself.

"Why was that?"

Hasley barely kept in a groan of annoyance. She may not know why the voice suggested she go with Amic Keyholder, but she knew it wouldn't be to conduct a long interview about fresh wounds. Hasley counted to three in her head and focused on Amic's voice. It wouldn't be much longer until they reached his home and she could rest. Maybe then, what she was seeing with her eyes would match up with the ambient sounds of the carriage on the road. Amic would be her anchor in the cabin, for now.

"Why was that?" Amic repeated. James continued to watch, looking back and forth between them as they spoke. Amic had far fewer questions to ask James than Hasley. Maybe that bothered him, but as of yet he hadn't expressed it. Instead, he followed the conversation in silence.

"She was keeping secrets, of course. She couldn't get close to others. We only became friends because I pursued it," Hasley admitted.

Her persistence had paid off then. Little did she know at the time, Ember would also become the only friend in her life. All other connections seemed to fall away from Hasley, she wasn't sure why. Given what was going on with her now, that was for the best.

"What did she tell you about her life?"

Hasley wondered if she should be saying anything at all. Even with what little she knew, Hasley had more knowledge about the heir to the throne than almost everyone in Ashkadance. The voice within her remained silent.

"She said her moms died, that's all she ever told me for a long time. We didn't talk about her personal life often."

The angry part of Hasley simmered, thinking again about how she could have done better by her friend. Hasley closed her eyes in pain, but the conflicting images assaulted her instead. She did not see the inside of the carriage or the darkness between her lids, instead dark waters and the smell of salt was in the air.

"Didn't you think that was odd and press her?" Amic asked, pushing in his own way.

He too wanted to know what Aaleia and Mutrien supposedly needed to impart on him through Hasley. His thoughts were more impatient than her own.

That question set Hasley's mood successfully over to the dark.

She snapped her eyes open again and positioned

herself in the direction of his voice. He flickered in her vision.

"Look, I don't know how many friends you have, but when they are clearly traumatized and private about something, yeah you occasionally push. If they freeze up, freak out, stop answering, and ignore you for a few days every time you ask then you stop asking. Flaming stars, you are irritating me. I am flaming losing my mind over here, trying to keep my eyes focused so that I am not drifting off into the ocean. Okay?"

She let out an exasperated breath and closed her eyes. The images resurfaced, and she opened them again. It was pointless, if the gods were telling her something, she couldn't stop it. She steadied herself and straightened her posture. This was not the time to let go of all manners and decorum.

Hasley had too much at stake and the stubborn part of her that got her in this carriage was going to see this mission through. Preferably with her mind intact.

She opened her mouth to apologize and start the conversation over again, but he spoke before she had the chance.

"You aren't old enough to have seen or at least, remember, the ocean. What do you see?"

She realized her slip and her heart beat faster. James was looking at her as well, rapt in attention.

"Is this one of your visions?" James asked. Hasley wouldn't call them visions, but she nodded as it was close enough.

"I haven't seen the ocean in person, but I recognize it. Ever since we got in the carriage today I've been seeing water, a large body of it, the blue sky, and sand. It comes in and out of my vision..." Hasley admitted. The small sliver of the ocean she had seen above the wall when standing at the higher points of Mount Pietan did not compare to this.

"There is a reason you were told to come on this mission with us," James said, speaking again. He patted her shoulder from across the space and said, "we'll figure out what it is soon enough."

Amic was quiet for a moment, looking at Hasley closely.

"You see sand?" he asked, grabbing that detail.

Hasley nodded.

Amic's mouth thinned and his posture tightened. That little detail meant something. Hasley would find out herself soon enough.

EIGHT

IT'S EASY

The carriage dropped them off in front of Amic Keyholder's home, but that was not their destination. Hasley stopped to admire its unique architecture, so unlike the keyholder's residence in Firetop. The peiradoone stone walls were painstakingly painted a rich tan not unlike her vision of the beach. As it was a difficult material to work with, this was already a surprise. Other than that, it had a domed roof.

"You can get settled in later," Amic said as he gestured for her and James to follow them.

The coachman went about taking their bags into the house. Amic's hands twitched at his side as he led them through the surrounding forest, the path they needed distinguished only by two clay pots upon entering. They did not have to walk long before it was clear they had arrived.

Beyond the thicket of trees was the pure white of the wall. A wraith flew down from atop of the trees and landed on Amic's shoulder as if it had been waiting. It's leg stuck out and Amic reached for the tiny scrawl of paper attached there.

"This is what I have to show you," Amic said as he unfurled the note.

"A wraith?" Hasley asked as she took in makeshift camp, and the uncharacteristically affectionate wraith on his shoulder.

"No," he said with a laugh.

"Over there," he gestured beyond the trees on the left, "is an elaborate tubing system for sending synthetic dragon blood over the wall. This, on the other hand," he scratched the wraith's chin, "is a message from my son from beyond the wall."

Amic barreled through his explanation despite Hasley's shocked expression. James seemed to latch on to the dragon blood, inching closer to where Amic had gestured. Between the trees, she could make out people carrying large objects.

"My son came from Faeinto to find me and we've been sending letters to each other by wraith over the wall. He brought the synthetic dragon blood, so the resistance can create weapons of blood fire."

Blood fire in small doses could be snuffed out, but left unchecked and in large doses would burn eternally. It could not be drowned by water. It wasn't uncommon in older inns to have one or two blood fire torches that they used to fuel their hearth. Otherwise, blood fire was reserved for the two palaces. One palace was in Azororion where Ember now lived, the other in Cruelindime where typically the Dragon Matron lived.

As far as Ashkadance knew, there were no pure full-sized dragons left. The blood of the wraiths and anchoris didn't have the same effect.

Men and women pushed carts full of barrels across the clearing. They disappeared down the path that led back to the keyholder's house. James turned to follow, already asking questions of the people he didn't know. His eyes were alight with excitement, feeling his purpose in these dangerous materials. Hasley felt jealous of his confidence.

How did Amic's son get barrels of dragon's blood? Synthetic or otherwise, she didn't see how that was possible.

"And that's it, it's that easy to talk to someone over

the wall and bring objects over to?" Hasley asked in disbelief.

How could it be so simple to contact people outside the wall? Sending wraiths shouldn't work with how tall the wall was. Amic pulled out writing supplies from a fallen down log before them and wrote two short words. Amic patted the small wraith, scratching behind its ear. The demi-dragon chirped and left with the short scribbled note. The note read:

I'm here.

The wall was so steep that the wraith grew small in their sights before they saw it turn over to the other side.

"No, it's not that easy," Amic said wryly as he watched the wraith fly away. "The person has to already be waiting on a boat or the small coastline right outside the wall when you send the wraith. You can't send a wraith over blindly. Wraiths can't fly far enough to reach the other kingdoms across the water."

"And the blood?" Hasley asked, looking to the shimmering barrels men and women were loading into the back of a carriage.

"It's not real blood from dragons, of course, it's created to mimic it. My son left and came back a few times over the year, but four months ago he brought someone else with him. This man told us how to make a pump that brings the fake dragon blood over the wall safely. It took several attempts to get the tubing the right length. Over a thousand feet of it to reach the other side with enough slack to connect to the matching pump they have on the coast..." he paused in thought. "We almost have enough of the blood."

"Enough for what? This isn't enough?" Hasley asked. Those few barrels were already more than she had ever seen.

Amic ignored the question, or didn't hear her, it was unclear as he shook thoughts from his head.

"Many people died putting this together, including the man who helped my son, before we got the process correct. I thank Aaleia and Mutrien every day that I hear from my son and know that he is safe."

"How did you know he was there?" she asked.

"He docked outside first and then sent the wraith over. Like his mother used to," Amic said.

The docks, her subconscious whispered.

"How does the royal family not know?" Hasley asked.

"The closest guard towers can't see beyond this area of the wall, it's a blind spot."

"That's lucky," Hasley commented.

"No, it's intentional. My pair, when she was alive, she was a friend of Karwyn's, and by association knew the Queen. I moved our community home and meeting area as close to the wall as possible when it was under construction. My pair was pregnant and on the other side visiting family in Faeinto when the wall was completed. They didn't let her back in, but she would travel to the wall to visit and we'd speak to each other this way in secret. Her foresight in telling me about the blindspots and that we should be close to it felt like divine intervention."

Amic paused as he recalled the memory of his lost pair. His eyes grew misty.

"The fact that I was able to talk to her again, despite the odds put against us, astonishes me every day. I'll always be grateful for that additional time with her."

Hasley couldn't help but wonder if it was an intervention, like the priestess said her messages were. It felt miraculous, with purpose, that they continued to see each other despite the wall. Yet, Hasley's message was still unclear.

"When she stopped visiting and sending letters, that's when I truly committed to the resistance, assuming the worst. I didn't know what else to do. I didn't even know what happened until a year ago when my son showed up old enough to sail his own boat and send me a letter. She died when he was ten."

The memory hurt him, he moved back and forth on his feet and looked away.

Hasley did not know what it was like to experience the loss of a pair, but she could imagine the pain. This situation was different from a natural death, however, as Amic and his pair had been physically separated for years before it happened. It seemed out of the realm of possibility, yet it was true. There was a lot about life that she had thought she knew.

She was wrong about so much.

NINE

GOLD

Hasley's energy began to drain and she almost sat down on the log before Amic, but decided against it. It was worse enough that she had told him about the voices and her visions. She didn't need another reason to seem weak or out of control. While here, she would be poised and take back any sense of dignity she had. His son was on the other side of the wall and his pair dead, he deserved her attention.

She looked up at the wall and its insurmountable height. It was so tall that no tree could reach it, no ladder could be made long enough. She could imagine it, the danger of the explosive blood going over the wall. One mistake and it would douse the resistance members below it. She could almost smell the burnt flesh of those lost.

While they waited for the reply from his son, Amic showed her how the tubing worked. He opened an empty barrel to show her the lining that was supposed to keep the blood more stable. He used special silver lined gloves when examining it before depositing the gloves back into his pocket.

"The resistance have been surveying the wall for weaknesses we can exploit. It's just about finding how and who can tie the plan and the people together around the idea. Many of the resistors are wary of taking a big step like this, but the right push will help them come around to the idea."

Hasley nodded, feeling similar qualms. Wanting the wall to come down and actually making it happen was a very different matter. Seeing the blood ominously slush in the barrels made her head swim. It was such a deep red it looked more black in tone. It glittered, but not like a jewel would have. This didn't feel like her purpose.

Hasley's eyes followed the sway of the trees. She stared up into their canopies, the moving leaves calming her thoughts. It felt harder to keep her mind focused.

The wraith chirped again, sounding far away, and

before Hasley could pinpoint where it came from, it soared down at her through the same trees.

He smiled, used to the sight of the creature coming with news from his son. Hasley had, of course, seen many wraiths before, but none that used its body in such a way to reach peak speed. Its wings were tucked in, face down at an angle that made it look like a shooting star. She supposed that wraiths that needed to send messages from each side of the wall would have better learned speed than the local wraiths she was used to.

The voice spoke softly, whispering in her mind to pay attention to what was happening.

He is yours. He is yours.

Who, the wraith?

Its small slim body tightened to go faster as it plummeted towards the ground. It pulled back the last second and spread its wings with another chirp, as if having fun, and landed on Amic's shoulders. The wraith stuck out its leg for Amic to take the letter before hopping onto Hasley's shoulder.

"Ah!" Hasley was startled as she felt the sharpness of its claws on her skin. The wraith wiggled and smelled her hair curiously. She must have imagined that, why would a wraith be that friendly?

"I've gotten used to wearing thicker shirts," Amic

said by way of apology as he unfurled the letter. It was longer than the quick notes Hasley would send to Ember. He skimmed the page before starting from the beginning to re-read the first few lines. Hasley felt curious, wanting to know more about the man that set up camp on the other side of the wall. He was someone who already seemed to defy what most people were capable of.

It's him. It's him. It's him. The voice told her and her heart quickened.

"Can I see?" Hasley asked. She didn't wait for the answer and her impulses forced her to abruptly take the letter from his hands.

"Hey," Amic protested. Before he could take it back from her, she set eyes on his son's wide looping handwriting. She read the letter hungrily, feeling his simple words as if they were written for her.

> *Hi Dad,*
>
> *How was your trip? What did the priestesses want to show you?*
>
> *The water has started to get colder, I find myself sticking my feet in almost daily. Sitting on the sand instead of the boat, I'm better able to focus my thoughts, as if being closer to the wall were medicine. I wonder if this has to do with*

exposure to the synthetic blood. Maybe being close to it for too long has impacted me.

Do you think that could be it? I don't know how Faeinto puts the blood together, it's a guarded secret, but maybe there are compounds in it that could impact the mind. Of course the secrecy is expected. As a trader, I understand the power of knowing something other people don't and being able to set a higher price, but I sometimes wonder what their goals are. Why give it to Ashkadance for free when they charge Grydagia a premium that is so steep that only the royal family can afford it?

The men left for another shipment, but they should be back soon from the refuel ship. I'll let you know when I can see them on the horizon. This should be the last of the shipments, now we just need to put the plan in action.

Have you talked to the dragon daughter yet?

I can't wait to finally meet you in person. I wish Mom was here. She'd be so proud of you.

See you soon dad,

Arsenio

Hasley's eyes widened as she read the letter again, hands trembling.

"Hasley, your skin..." Amic whispered. His tone was no longer of angry surprise, but one of wonder.

She impatiently looked up at him, feeling an overwhelming urge to not be disturbed. To be alone with these few pieces of paper. Something caught the corner of her eye as her head moved up, a shimmer of gold. She looked at her hands, then her arms, down to her exposed legs.

She was gold. Well, not exactly gold. But she shimmered in a halo of golden light. It was not the sparkling explosive gold of the fating, but an aura of it. She was radiating it. As soon as it came, the color faded. She dropped the letter and her feet began to shake.

"I don't understand," she said.

But she did. The voice knew. Hasley picked up the letter and clutched it to her chest. The reason for the voices, for the drive to this particular part of the wall above all others, her fate was on the other side of it. Hasley was not fateless.

She just couldn't get to him.

Go to the docks, the voice had said on the last day she was with her parents.

"I think I do," Amic said. He handed her a fresh spiral of paper and a writing utensil.

"Take this and write to my son, tell him about yourself, and what happened."

Tears began to gather in Hasley's eyes as she took the paper.

Hi Arsenio, I'm Hasley.

I met your father at Mount Pietan. I was called to be there and we found each other. I had a feeling, this knowing, and a voice. The voice told me to come to this spot.

Then, I read your letter and the world changed.

I've been away from home for two weeks now. I left everything behind. It sounds like you did too.

I'm glowing gold, I believe because you are my pair. Are you glowing too?

Hasley Jeweler

PART 2
NEVER THE SAME

TEN

LETTERS IN THE DIVIDE

Hasley,

We found each other. I have never been so scared and happy at the same time.

I wish I could become one with the blood pumped up this wall and reform on the other side, a whole human for you. I wish I had miles of your words to read. I wish I was touching the hands that wrote them.

I wish for so much, but mostly for you to be free from pain and the voices.

I feel almost more desperate now that I know you are there. The voices feel louder. Yes, I had them too. I was afraid to tell my dad because there was nothing he could do on that side. At least, there was nothing he could do yet. But it seems he helped solve it without knowing, by trusting that you needed to be here.

Tell me about yourself. Tell me all of the important parts. Or even the little things, like what you do first thing when you open your eyes.

I am Arsenio, son of Amic Keyholder and Lane Trader. I haven't met my dad in person yet, I was born on the other side of the wall and raised in Faeinto. About a year ago I became a trader, feeling the urge to travel and wanting to take the path my mom did to communicate with Dad. That underlying feeling though must have been for this, so I could meet you. We were meant to be for each other. If this wall weren't here, we may have met on these docks or in the markets. I would have brought exotic jewels from Faeinto, and you would have been selling your wares..

Did something change in your life a year ago too?

After some time, I found my way to the spot my mom told me about as a child. I know she used to come here, but for fear of me getting hurt and discovered, I wasn't allowed. She passed away, so I came anyway.

After one of the leaders of Faeinto discovered what I was doing, they helped me bring the synthetic blood here. They wanted to help my father liberate Ashkadance. I had thought the blood was hurting me, that helping transport it was influencing me somehow. But I know now, it was because I was waiting for you.

I can't wait to get to know you.

Arsenio

Hasley looked up from the letter, gold filtering in and out of her vision. The workers that helped Arsenio with the tubing and transportation surrounded her. They stared in wonder at her golden light and the letter. Tears rolled from a few eyes as it faded away. She began to cry too.

Hasley sat on that log all day, letters transported back and forth. Bliss and loss flowed in waves across her day, with men and women Arsenio trusted watching and leaving. She was like an animal, trapped in her mind, ecstatic to be loved and then completely lost in moments. But for that first day, she was always watched. As time passed, Amic left and returned with supplies for her.

"I don't suppose I can convince you to come back to my home?" Amic asked, a bundle in his arms.

Hasley shook her head no, too exhausted for words. She would not leave this place, not with her heart so close by.

Amic smiled a half-smile and said, "I thought as much. Here."

He unrolled his bundle and handed her blankets, a small pillow, and some snacks.

She took the soft blankets in her hands and wrapped them around her legs. She felt the impulse to bring them up to her chest, but she wanted to have her hands free and ready to write. As if he knew her thoughts, Amic pulled out more stacks of paper from his jacket and left them in a pile on the log nearby.

"I'll have James come back soon with a lantern and more food for dinner. It's getting late. If you change your mind, come back home okay?"

At the mention of home, Hasley's eyes widened. She left her home over two weeks ago now. He seemed to notice and crouched before her. His hand came to her shoulder.

"Your home will always be with me and my son, okay Hasley? Whether that be temporarily here at the wall, or my home, or in the community home a short distance away. You have support and somewhere to go, no matter what, okay?"

"Okay," she whispered

Hasley realized for the first time that being fated with Arsenio also meant that she was tied to Amic's life too. Maybe when she and Arsenio saw each other in person, she would feel normal again. She would feel safe. Then, Arsenio could meet her parents and they could move to Borderain. That is, assuming they didn't move to Faeinto, where Arsenio grew up.

When she was alone again, she pulled the blank pieces of paper closer to her. They rested half under her leg, an impulse to protect them from possible blowing wind, even though there wasn't much wind through the dense forest of trees.

She wrote her next letter, knowing he was waiting for it on the other side. She imagined his back against the wall in the same position as hers and smiled at the image.

Arsenio,

I am as broken as ever. My whole life I've been chasing perfection. Chasing a life that I could never meet. I was best friends with the princess. Even though I didn't know her true identity, I knew that she was special. As for what happened last year, around the time you started trading, that's when I started my apprenticeship with her at a jeweler in town.

As for who I am? I am nice, but not the nicest. I am pretty, but not the prettiest. I am clever, but was never the smartest in the class. I was never the best, not in a single thing I did. But I was the best clerk at least, while I was in the jewelry apprenticeship. I didn't actually make any of the jewelry, I only sold it and helped keep things orderly.

Being without my best friend has been hard. She was gone so suddenly and I hadn't yet had the courage to tell her what was happening to me. The voices then grew stronger.

I didn't want much from my future, other than the typical things. I wanted a purpose I didn't hate. I wanted a pair. I wanted a family.

And here you are. And I'm lower than low. Undeserving of a pair. You should not feel pain like this. Knowing you are on the other side of this wall, hurting, because I am not there to stop it, is worse. More painful than any other inadequacy.

I want to save you, but how can I if I can't even save myself?

I left my family without a word. I left my purpose without a word. Ember never shared her secrets with me and I never told her mine. Maybe I deserve this. I deserve this bed of dirt. But you? You do not. I want to take your pain from you and swap with you, so that you are here with your father and I am alone on the other side.

Hasley

DESPITE THE LENGTH of her message, and the length of his reply, barely any time had passed before the wraith descended before her once more.

Hasley,

How wrong you are. You are deserving of love, hope, fate, joy. Never compare yourself to anyone or anything else. This love between us will only get bigger. You are not going to save me. I'm going to save myself. Then you are going to save you. And together, we'll help save a kingdom.

The kingdom is not Ashkadance, by the way. The kingdom is our future. For each fated pair finds in each other what they need, and I plan to do big things in this life.

Please, don't despair. Don't blame yourself. How could you possibly blame yourself for us being separated? It is not logical. I like to call myself a logical person with a pinch of unrealistic goal achieving. I see how other people should approach their life, then I add my version of logic, and make something very exciting out of my ideas.

I'd like to bring you into this magic. Together we have our logic because logical and realistic are subjective words. They only mean what we decide it means.

You are the best, Hasley. You are my best. Together we can do anything.

I'll be strong for you today, and tomorrow we can swap. Does that sound like a good idea? We'll balance this pain, shoulder the voices until we can make them stop.

When we are together, what is the first thing you want to do?

-A

The voice in Hasley's head calmed down when

reading his letters. It didn't insist, weigh down, or bleed into her subconscious with suggestions of things she didn't want to do. How could this be? How can someone become fated to someone they haven't met? Could her true purpose be outside these walls?

It must be. Her future lay outside of the physical wall as well as the emotional one she built for herself. Out there she was without regulations, perfectionism, and lies.

Maybe this was Aaelia and Mutrien's will, for Hasley to learn outside of perfection, to meet a boy that was not afraid to be big and honor her too.

Arsenio,

I like that plan. We can take turns. We can share our fears and feel safe. We can do this together.

As the sun turns in to sleep and the moon comes out to play, I wish I was in your arms. That is what I want to do when I see you. I want to hold you and have you hold me. That's what I want more than anything. We'll have that, soon.

What is planned so far? What is your part in it and how can I help?

-Hasley

Hasley lay against the wall that night, feeling the cold stone against her back. She burrowed deeper into the blankets Amic provided. She couldn't leave this place, her body and mind refused her. The only comfort was her knowing he was on the other side. She was not alone, not like she thought, and she would never be again.

A chirp came from above her and she turned bleary eyes up. The chirp was happier than that morning, more musical somehow. The wraith slowed its flight and landed softly beside her. It stuck out its leg and tilted its head to survey her. Hasley greedily took the letter and felt the warmth of the fating again, spreading through her soul with relief. The message was shorter this time than their letters back and forth the past day.

Her name is Amalthea, I raised her since she was born. She'll keep you company tonight.

A tear rolled down Hasley's face and the demi-dragon hopped closer. She leaned into the crook of Hasley's neck and breathed a hot sigh onto her skin with a purr. Hasley wrapped a tentative arm and blanket around the creature as her glow lessened, grateful for the companionship. Amalthea's talons grazed Hasley's skin by mistake as she snuggled in. Hasley winced before the wraith pulled its arms tighter into its chest to keep its talons back.

"Thanks," Hasley whispered to the wraith.

It chirped back and cuddled closer as a raindrop fell from the sky.

ELEVEN

A DAUGHTER IN FATE

Hasley awoke to James shaking her shoulder. He brought warm food for her and a change of clothes. She shivered in the morning air, uncovering herself from the damp blankets. She had never dried in the night, even when the rain stopped. The early morning moisture and puddles from the rain surrounded her. Her teeth clacked together uncontrollably James grew wide-eyed in alarm.

"I'm going to make a fire," he said as he turned away from her.

Hasley felt a weight on her shoulders, momentarily confused why. The memory came back to her seconds later. Amalthea, the wraith that had sent their letters across the wall, had kept Arsenio's promise to stay the night with her. Amalthea curled around her neck like a scarf, head resting behind a curtain of her hair. Hasley pulled strands back, tying her blue hair into a knot and away from the demi-dragon.

Amalthea stirred, stretching out her claws subconsciously as she awoke. Hasley flinched, a new scratch on her growing collection. A purr emitted from its chest before Amalthea jumped from her shoulders and onto the ground. It chirped a few times at James before jumping up to full flight. She smiled up at the sky, knowing it went to check on Arsenio.

"An unexpected day, huh?" James asked as he got a fire ready to warm them. Had it only been a day since she arrived with James and Amic at Borderain? It felt like one day and a lifetime.

"We'll have a few more unexpected days before we're okay again," Hasley answered. She dropped the blankets behind her and stood.

"You really think we'll be okay?" James asked skeptically as the pit ignited.

"No," she answered as she stood on frigid legs.

She sat down before the fire. Her toes sunk into the dirt, for once not caring about appearance. She buried her ideas of a perfect life the night before. While she'd never be totally free of that expectation, she knew life felt much more exciting with a crack in the veneer.

Amalthea was back again.

I missed you.

Three words on paper that pushed her heart out of her chest.

"Has that happened with every single letter?" James asked as he watched the gold fade away.

Hasley nodded, no longer able to speak.

It continued this way for days, or so she believed. Hasley subconsciously logged the days based on James' visits for breakfast, but she didn't bother knowing exact dates. What did time matter anymore? What she experienced with Arsenio was all-consuming. The seconds between speaking with him were all that mattered.

Until one morning, James didn't come for breakfast. Hasley waited snuggled in her makeshift bed with Amalthea before her hunger grew too much for her to ignore. She stood up and re-tied the cloth around her waistband tighter and put on her shoes. While she waited to see if James would appear, Hasley tried to tame her bed head with her fingers.

Somewhat satisfied, she used the small bucket of water she had close by to rinse her face.

After becoming more presentable, her friend still did not come. With little other option, Hasley wrote a quick note and sent it with Amalthea over the wall.

Good morning. I'll be right back, I have to go to your dad's house for a few minutes.

Taking one last look behind her, Hasley took her first step away from her campsite. She walked what she hoped was the right path, looking for the tall orange clay pots she had seen that first day she entered the forest with Amic and James.

Hasley stood at the edge of the road, taking a deep breath. It had only been a few days and she felt completely foreign to the world. She reached up again to her hair before putting her hand back down. There wasn't anything she could do about it now, she had to keep moving. Thankfully, Amic's home wasn't far.

"How can I help you?" a woman asked when Hasley walked up the steps to the door. She had bright red hair, dark skin, and was significantly taller than Hasley. She stood beside the entrance, greeting citizens of the province that came to speak to Amic without an appointment.

"I'm Hasley Jeweler, can you tell me where Amic and James are?" she said, self conscious of the spot of dirt she just noticed on her hand. She put her hands behind her back and stood straighter.

"A pleasure to meet you, Hasley. Amic told me all about you. My name is Sandra Clerk. Would you like me to show you to your room?"

Hasley blinked, not understanding the question. "I have a room?"

"Of course, you are Amic's daughter in fate after all. Not that many know that, but I do. I work closely with Amic in his efforts. Come with me, Hasley, I'll show you to your room and let him know to meet you."

Sandra smiled warmly at Hasley and beckoned her forward. Hasley hesitantly followed her into the building. Inside was an open dining space, ceiling-to-floor white columns, and small blue geometric tiles on the floor.

"It's a sight, isn't it? The bedrooms are along this way," Sandra continued down to a side door. They walked down a long hallway to the end and turned left. Another row of doors continued on from there. Sandra stopped in front of the fourth door.

"This is the one," she said and turned the knob.

Hasley gasped and covered her mouth. Inside was a four poster bed with light pink sheets and a pile of fluffy white pillows. The floor was carpeted, with a small writing table beside the window. It was much bigger than her room at home. The way the light shined through the sheer white window curtains and onto the bed made Hasley want to lay down and sleep in its warmth.

"I'll go fetch the boys," Sandra said and turned to leave.

Hasley walked further into the room and sat on the edge of the bed. Her bag, which up until this point she had entirely forgotten about, laid on the small end table beside the bed. Overwhelmed and exhausted, she fell backwards onto the covers and closed her eyes.

"Hasley. Hasley can you hear me?"

Hasley could feel her body shaking, but her mind couldn't register the feeling as belonging to her. She opened her eyes and instead of the bedroom she had been in moments prior, Hasley was on a beach. She saw sand, the glittering water beyond it, and in the distance a vessel tied to decaying wood and a broken-down dock.

"Hasley, wake up," the familiar voice said again. Her body felt movement, arms on her shoulders and a hand to her brow, but she stayed put. Hasley wore a white dress and it blew behind her in the breeze.

She sighed and thought, *this is where I want to be.*

That is where you should be, the voice of her fatelessness answered.

TWELVE

MEANING IN PAIN

Hasley reunited with her physical body in a jolt. She was back in the room Sandra said was hers, with two concerned faces staring back at her.

"Oh thank Aaleia, you are okay," Amic said in relief. His voice quivered uncharacteristically.

"What's wrong?" Hasley asked, confused why they were concerned by her napping. Then, the vision slowly returned to her. It wasn't a dream, was it?

"You were staring at the ceiling. We tried to talk to you, we tried to shake you, but you were unresponsive. It was pretty scary. How do you feel? What did you see?" James asked.

"I was by the water again, but this time I think I saw Arsenio's boat," Hasley explained. "I was there, but I also wasn't at the same time, it was confusing yet peaceful."

"We'll have to see if Arsenio saw the same thing," Amic mused, coughing into his hand and standing up from the bed. He straightened invisible wrinkles in his jacket.

"I'm sorry I wasn't there for breakfast, Hasley, we were strategizing and I lost track of time," James explained.

"Of course, I understand, James," Hasley said lightly and also stood from the bed. She stood from the bed.

"Speaking of Arsenio, this room is for the both of you. Once this mess is over." He gestured around the space before beginning to pace.

"What were you strategizing over?" Hasley asked curiously. Despite just standing up, the lack of food and comfortable sleep made her feel dizzy. She sat in the chair at the writing desk.

"Getting allies. Amic can explain, right?" James looked to Amic, who nodded. "I'll get you some food and be right back."

James left the room in a rush. Amic opened his mouth to talk. Before he could get a word out, Hasley said, "thank you, so very much."

Amic's brows furrowed. "For what?" he asked.

"For the room, for the care and kindness you've shown me. For everything," Hasley said and gestured wide to encompass where they stood.

"You're my family now, Hasley. You deserve a place to call your own," he said.

Hasley felt an emotional lump in her throat. She already had a place, and a family, waiting for her back in Firetop. When she made the choice to leave it all, she didn't imagine she would find another. But here she was, so close to both.

"Well, thank you all the same," she said with a genuine smile.

Amic flushed and cleared his throat. "Anyway, the problem we are facing is in finding allies, something to unify the different pockets of rebellion around the idea of using the synthetic dragon blood. We don't have enough numbers yet for the united strike we need to weaken the wall enough to be rid of it for good."

"What do you think would help bring in numbers?" she asked.

"People are scared. They know they want change, but the idea of it is too abstract to risk their lives for it. They need something concrete, something physical to show that they are right to place their hopes in it," Amic mused.

A memory flashed in Hasley's mind. On the day

she partially fated to Arsenio, the strangers carting away barrels witnessed what happened to her and cried. In fact, most people that saw her had cried, Amic and James included.In that moment, she was made of pure hope.

"Would what is happening to me, a fating kept apart by the wall, provide enough of a symbol?" she asked hesitantly. Her gut twisted at the thought of sharing more of her pain, but she also knew this was an opportunity to further her purpose.

He stopped his pacing and turned to her. "Maybe, why do you ask?"

"I wouldn't mind," Hasley began. She started to lie, then chose honesty instead. "If you think that people seeing our interrupted fating will help the cause, then bring key people to see me in the woods. Ask Ember, even. It's time she knew the whole truth."

Amic placed a fatherly hand on her shoulder. "Only if you are comfortable with it. If you decide afterward you don't want to have any more visitors, that is okay. You can change your mind about your involvement in this anytime, okay?"

Hasley nodded. James knocked on the door and entered with a tray. While she ate the fresh fruit and sandwich he brought, Amic and James discussed the idea and who should come to see her. She tried to listen, but she felt drained of social energy.

Each bite felt like a strange torture. Hasley felt she needed to get back to the wall, back to Amalthea and Arsenio and their letters, but she also needed strength. She held out to the last bite, downing a drink and standing back up.

"I have to go, I can't stay any longer."

James stopped his conversation and followed her to the door. "I'll help you get back to the camp," he said.

"It's fine," Hasley said in a rush, the door knob already in her hands.

"You are always welcome here," Amic called to her as she rushed down the hall.

THIRTEEN

EMBER DRAGON DAUGHTER

On this particular day, Hasley decided to wear the dress she had left her home in. She had avoided wearing it most days, instead keeping to the clothes Amic and James brought her. Today she could imagine meeting him in person with more detail, as if the dress reminded her what it would have been like to be normal again. The dress had stains and was not as cute as it had been before her adventures thus far, but she wanted to wear it.

Hasley groggily pulled the blanket around herself as she heard the sound of approaching footsteps. She thought it must be lunch based emptiness of her stomach, but she couldn't muster up the energy to look up.

Another letter would be coming soon, and she only had the energy for that.

"Because of her," Amic said distantly. Multiple gasps sounded.

Ah, it couldn't be James then. She did not want to be on show today. Over the past week she had secured more than a dozen people's help in the coming demolition. She knew it was important work, and it seemed to be helping, but it drained her like nothing else. This was supposed to be a private pain.

But this was no stranger. Hasley felt a wave of relief as she met the eye of her best friend and future ruler. Her smile quickly broke into a sob.

"Hasley," Ember called and ran to her.

They collapsed together onto the floor, arms wrapped around each other. Ember's black and rainbow reflecting hair was shorter now, which surprised Hasley. Life back in the palace must have changed Ember's confidence, as surely as Hasley was irrevocably different. In the weeks since they've seen each other, everything was different.

"I'm sorry," Hasley said between hacking breaths. She buried her face into Ember's neck.

"Why would you be sorry, Hasley? You have done nothing wrong. I'm the one that is sorry. I failed you,"

Ember whispered. Ember held tighter to her best friend, brushing her dirty hair with soft fingers.

"I knew. I knew I was sick. I couldn't tell you. I... I..." Hasley's fumbled for the right words.

She felt sorry for so many things, for the jealousy, for the need to be number one, for not writing to her or confiding in her.

"It'll be okay," a man said from beside Amic. He inched closer to them. "We can help you."

Hasley even felt sorry for not knowing this man, as it must have been her best friend's pair, Noorworth Knight. Amic had told her that shortly before meeting Hasley he had met Ember and her fated knight at her debut ball. The one Hasley should have been at.

"If we take down the wall, we can," Amic said to Ember and the curly haired man with her. Ember turned to him from her seat on the floor. "What do you mean?"

"Her pair is outside that wall, right now," Amic said matter-of-factly.

Amic pointed to the spot right behind Hasley's head, as if her pair was actually there this moment. If only he could hear them, know that the dragon daughter was here. He would want to meet her, as he had met the rulers of his own kingdom once.

Ember held her hand to her mouth, too shocked to speak. A tear ran down her friend's face.

"I'm sorry," Hasley whispered again, this time to herself. She pushed her back flat to the wall. Her friend was here, but she couldn't focus on her. She couldn't focus on much but her next letter.

"How can you know that?" Ember's pair asked Amic. Of course, the question was needed. But there wasn't any way to answer it, they wouldn't understand until they witnessed it themselves.

As if waiting for the right moment, Amalthea flew in from above and landed onto Hasley's shoulder. Amalthea nuzzled her bowed head like a pet, scales meeting blue hair, and Hasley looked to her with a smile. A real happy smile, she felt like the wraith was part of her family now. It helped her feel like she was normal, ironically.

Hasley reached for the scroll tied to the wraith's leg and opened it greedily. Her skin brightened from the inside out as she read. A soft yellow cast seemed to bring her to life as she absorbed the words. She was warm and fulfilled once more, her heart healing.

"What's happening?" Ember whispered.

"Come closer and see," Amic said. The three sat before Hasley on the ground as she fished for something to write with from her dress pocket. She wrote on the opposite side of the letter feverishly.

The wraith hopped down, her long thin tail brushing the grass. As Hasley finished her scribbles, it stuck out its leg and accepted the letter. Amalthea adjusted her stance and with a proud chirp flew fast into the sky. They tilted their heads up to watch the small demi-dragon disappear over the wall.

"But wraiths can't fly over the wall to deliver letters," Ember's pair said in disbelief. They were told this fact their whole life and yet it was not true. There were many truths that seemed only partially true when years passed by.

"Oh, but they can, Noorworth Knight," Amic said. "You just have to have someone at exactly that spot on the other side waiting. If no one is there, the wraith's circle back. The water is too far for them to cross, but they can visit the eroding coast and old docks on the other side if they have a reason to."

"Someone is out there," Ember echoed his meaning, staring at Hasley instead of the wall.

Hasley kept her face upturned, eyes bright and smile wide with the golden glow. But as the seconds passed, Hasley's skin lost its glow and her smile turned to a more-familiar frown. As if the light never appeared to her, tears welled up, and she looked back to the ground. She wrapped her arms around her legs as she buried her face in her lap.

"Who are you speaking to, Hasley?" Ember asked quietly, scared to disturb her.

"Arsenio," Hasley said between tears, her body quivered at the mention of his name aloud.

"My son," Amic elaborated. "She and my son experience bursts of the fating every day, then they feel it ripped from them."

"Help us," Hasley whispered.

She knew Ember was one of the few people that could help Amic and the resistance. In turn, she and Arsenio would be free. And she felt selfish for asking. Selfish for asking her friend of something so impossible. But if anyone could take the wall down, it was her.

"How?" Ember asked no one in particular. She didn't know how she could make things better, just like Hasley, but Amic seemed to.

"I have something else to show you," Amic said and led them away. Ember hugged her friend goodbye. Hasley hoped this wasn't the last time she'd see her. For what happened next, could be the end of them all.

Hasley drew back into herself, no longer capable of speech. She knew that Ember would now go to the dragon blood. She knew that she, Amic, James, and the resistance, would all come together. Hasley would try to help in any way she could.

But really, she knew all she could do was try to help herself and Arsenio before anyone else. No one should live this way. No fateless should be trapped in their bodies and minds, unable to reach their pair in the way that she could.

The wall separated families, loved ones, opportunity, and the very destiny outlined by the gods. Not even the sea was free of pain, it haunted her and Arsenio's visions. It was all severed by the royal family. And for what?

For a supposed mermaid feud, if history was to be believed. For safety. To keep the fatelessness from spreading. And yet, Hasley felt it was the cause of it all.

That night Ember returned and held her in her arms while Hasley cried. When Ember left right before dawn, Hasley felt a part of her heart heal.

FOURTEEN

WHERE IS HOME?

"I met her, Embrence Dragon Daughter," James said the next day at breakfast. "She said something very interesting about the synthetic dragon's blood."

Hasley stared at him, waiting for him to elaborate as she collected herself. Mornings felt both easier and harder, as if sleep replenished her physical energy, but zapped her of her mental energy from the long hours of separation from Arsenio. She had a feeling Arsenio slept as little as she did. Waking up in fits, yet wanting the other to rest. Thinking about it now, it seemed like a fruitless effort.

James continued, used to Hasley's divided attention.

"She said it isn't fake blood. She could sense that it

was real. They have a dragon on Faeinto, or at least, they used too. Maybe it's dead. You know, since we have all this blood here."

That statement did, however, catch Hasley's attention. Hasley didn't know what she could say or express. If there was a dragon out and about, Arsenio would have told her, wouldn't he? And Ember's ability to detect it was real, how could she be sure?

In her next letter, Hasley prodded the question.

> *What do you know of the synthetic dragon blood? How did they come about giving it to you? I'd love to know more about the kingdom you are from.*

Hasley attempted to soften the question, asking for more on his background. She did want to know more, it wasn't a lie, but the reason for bringing it up so bluntly wasn't necessarily how she would have done it.

> *I would love to tell you, Hasley. I also wondered when you'd ask.*
> *Faeinto is very different than what I know of Ashkadance. Less hard. More free-flowing. As you know, Faeinto is the home of the unicorns. We still have them, running free in the fields of*

our own royal family. Mother was a trader as well, though by necessity and not for the love of it. Travel between us and Grydagia is monitored. Those with ships need to be vetted, and it's harder to go in this direction than it looks.

Most of the people that attempted to come to Ashkadance-out of curiosity or a wild idea to liberate the kingdom on their own-turn around halfway through. The merfolk guard the sea near Ashkadance. It's not even that Faeinto doesn't allow it, it's all the merfolk.

The merfolk don't believe in meddling with the affairs of the kingdoms, and want each of them to choose their own path in their interpretation of Mutrien and Aaleia's vision.

My mother, on the other hand, had special permission from the merfolk to travel here. Not that she'd tell anyone about it but me. Her family didn't even know she came here. But she did need an excuse for her travels. Hence, the trading routes. It took me a few years to realize she was bad at trading. She didn't enjoy the profession, but I did. I don't know how she convinced the merfolk to let her through, but that favor extended to me when I was old enough. Maybe she told them the truth? Regardless, when I sail this way the merfolk simply move out of the way and let me pass.

I, however, wasn't as good at sailing as my mother was. So I needed to hire help running my ship. And eventually, one of the shipmates told someone and it spread. By my third visit to talk to Dad, the royal family was intervening and asking me for information.

I couldn't just pretend I wasn't able to come here. They already knew. And miraculously, they did want to help. They've been working on stock-piling extra of their faux dragon blood for years. They knew it was the only thing that could successfully crack through the peiradoone walls. It was some old war knowledge, passed on through the royal family line. The king sent me letters to pass on to Dad, who agreed to take the material before we even knew how to use it.

And that's how we ended up here. The only thing different about this story is now I refuse to leave. The Faeinto workers come and go on my ship and the merfolk let them through.

I don't know how they make the blood, it's a guarded secret. But they are charging Grydagia a premium for it, meanwhile, they are giving it to us for free.

I sometimes wonder, how will they ask us to pay for this favor in the future? But the royal family is forgiving and honest, maybe that's the unicorn influence in their blood. We'll have to see with time.

And you, my dear, would look very lovely in their braided hairstyles with silver trim woven in. For the royal family they weave in unicorn hair, but the rest of the kingdom has to get creative with ribbons and colorful thread.

I just realized you could have short hair or even hate braids. What do you look like? Wait, no, I'd like to see it with my own eyes. My eyes are grey, by the way. I'll give you that much.

Yours,
Arsenio

Hasley felt guilty as she read it, which was a very conflicting feeling to have while in the midst of their strange partial fatings. Each time the warmth comforted her and gave her peace, yet it was not as satisfying as she imagined it would be when it settled permanently.

With these interruptions, she didn't feel whole. She felt worse than when she was completely fateless, because this was an interruption on her soul. She decided that was a good way to describe it, as being interrupted. As a fateless, she felt invaded. As interrupted, she was incomplete.

But the guilt for assuming Arsenio must know more about the truth of the dragon's blood lingered with Hasley. He would tell her if dragons were walking around Faeinto, right?

This knowing him but not entirely was a stain on her conscience, one she couldn't wait to be rid of. But it would be over soon, Ember now knew the truth. She would help Amic in his plan and Hasley would be home again. Wherever that home may be.

Ember had been prepared to run away from her home at any moment. Hasley pretended not to notice that Ember always had spare clothing and extra food with her. Once she even glimpsed a knife in her bag. She knew her friend had secrets and a past she couldn't share, but Hasley would never have guessed her friend was the missing heir to the dragon throne.

For one thing, Ember never seemed like she wanted the things a crown would give. She was always hidden, separate, haunted. Before Ember's letters, Hasley thought that meant Ember knew she was the heir, that she had somehow escaped and was hiding. It turns out she was hiding from the world, but because of a deeper deception, she was told all her life. She thought her scales would endanger her family and lead to her death.

That turned out not too far from the truth. Ember couldn't possibly be the same girl she knew now. But which version of her friend did Hasley need, the one that knew how to hide in plain sight or the future queen of a dragon kingdom that no longer had dragons?

And now, which home did Hasley need? One that was familiar and included what pieces of her past that she could salvage, or one that was entirely new?

FIFTEEN

UNOPENED

Hasley shivered, a sheen of sweat slick on her skin. Coming slowly into conscious awareness, she re-adjusted her blankets to get warmer. She opened her eyes, realizing this was not the same blanket she went to bed with.

"Hi," a voice said to her left. Hasley turned over in bed and saw Sandra sitting in a chair next to her.

"Welcome back," Sandra said. She stood and pushed a tray closer to her on the bed. Hasley sat up and accepted the bowl of broth.

"What am I doing here?" Hasley asked and shivered again. She hoped the answer wasn't that she sleepwalked through a forest in the night.

"James found you ill this morning. You spent the night in the rain and dirt. You should've come over here, Hasley, we'd have kept you safe. But anyway, you seemed confused and couldn't stop sneezing and shivering so he carried you here. You slept about...." Sandra looked up to the ceiling, as if it had an answer.

"Six hours since you got here, I believe. It's well into the afternoon now," Sandra finished.

"No, no, does Arsenio know I'm here?" Hasley pushed away the food and blanket and tried to get out of bed.

"Of course he knows," Amic said as he strode in the room.

"He asked me to give you this." He held out a letter to her.

Hasley nearly fell as she eagerly reached for the letter and sat on the floor to read it. The grey baggy trousers she wore pooled at her ankles.

> *Hasley, the most important thing you can do for yourself is take care of your health. Both in your mind and your body. Please, if it is raining go to my dad's house. Hearing you were there all night in the cold broke my heart. Even I sometimes stay on my boat. It isn't as comfy as my dad's house, I'm sure, but it'll do.*
>
> *I'll miss you, but stay the day if you can. One day, we'll get to stay there together.*

-A

Hasley's smile faltered as the gold of the fating faded and she clutched the letter to her chest. She knew if the situation were reversed, she'd tell Arsenio the same thing. It didn't make it any easier for her to accept, but accept she must.

Hasley got back into bed and focused on what was right for her--rest, food, and sleep. But mostly sleep. She awoke to another tray of food carried by Sandra, so it must have been hours. Not long after Amic entered quietly, relieved to see her awake.

"James and I are working on updating your camp-site so that you are more comfortable," Amic said as he sat on the edge of her bed. Hasley sneezed and blew her nose.

"Can you make sure that there are open spaces for Amalthea to fly? I don't want her to be too boxed in," Hasley requested, braiding her hair as she talked.

"Of course, we thought you would like that and we're already building it that way. You'll have an open canopy draped over branches so that rain won't hit you if it came from straight above. The sides are open so Amalthea can fly in and out. It won't solve for rain coming in sideways, but we'll think of something or you can come join us on those days."

"Thank you," Hasley whispered and snuggled back down into the blankets.

"I have one more thing for you," Amic said and reached into his pocket. He pulled out a sealed envelope, weathered over many years.

"What is it?" she asked, feeling a surge of nervous energy.

"Lane gave this to me during one of her last visits. She told me that one day, we would be together again and we would give this sealed envelope to Arsenio and his pair when they met," he clutched the letter to his chest. "And that's you. It's meant for you two."

Hasley could feel the despair radiating off of him. "What's in it?" she asked gently.

"It holds her hopes and dreams for our growing family and stories from when she and I were first fated," Amic choked out, "All these years I thought about opening it, but I couldn't face it knowing that it is the last letter from her that I'll ever read."

Hasley couldn't imagine how he felt. With every letter she felt her pair ripped from her, but it was okay because she knew it wouldn't be forever. Amic's pain was infinite.

"When I saw you glow gold to his letter, it broke my heart. To know that you and my son would feel that same pain of separation, that I hadn't prevented it from happening to him by finding a way to take down this dragon's piss of a wall sooner." He sighed in regret.

"There is a whole kingdom worth of people who haven't solved this, or did nothing for they thought they had no power or right too. You found a way, and you are acting on it. Please don't be upset with yourself about it," she said.

Amic shook his head, seemingly not hearing her. "I thought about opening the letter then, hoping for comfort and advice for myself. But I couldn't do that to you two. It's for you and Arsenio to open once you are together. This time, I know it will happen soon."

He held out the letter but seemed unwilling to let it go. Hasley pulled him into a hug.

SIXTEEN

A GAME

"She's agreed with the timing! She writes that she had already been meeting the other resistors when she knew you were missing and she will continue to do so, but with the extra notice that she is endorsing the wall's destruction. We are working soon when the coordinated day will be, but I think they'll agree with my suggestion," Amic said the next day, coming into her newly made camp with James and another man she didn't know.

Amic's chest seemed to puff at the thought of his suggestion, so Hasley had to ask.

"I assume you mean Ember?" Hasley hedged, "And what was your suggestion?"

"For the explosion to happen during the Mutrien ball," Amic supplied.

He smiled with his teeth and crossed his arms, waiting for praise over the idea. Hasley sometimes forgot he was the oldest of their companions, only a little younger than her own parents. He seemed alive and youthful with them. It was almost as if he too was at the start of his life, looking for purpose and the fating, instead of the tragedy that was his separation from his pair.

"Guards and party guests will be busy with their revels, it was a good idea," the mystery man said. James turned to look at him, and the mystery man looked back at him with a twinkle in his eyes. They stood close, but not touching.

"Hi, I'm Hasley," she said, keeping her spot on the log and waiting for an introduction back. The way they looked at each other suggested something, but she wasn't sure of what. She rubbed her hands and held them near the fire. Despite the temperature being pleasant for everyone else, she felt cold in her limbs constantly. Goosebumps rose on her exposed arms.

"I'm Maroon, James' pair. We met yesterday. I was supposed to meet you, actually, but I saw James first," he said.

Hasley felt a clenching in her heart as sudden as a knife wound. Her and James had come here together, both out of sorts and part of the fateless. While Hasley knew her pair was waiting for her just beyond the wall, she felt left out now that James met his pair officially before her. It was as if their journey together as tortured compatriots was over, and she was left behind, wanting and alone.

Jealousy felt like an infected bug bite, an irritant that came up without warning and at the flip of a coin could root into her soul or heal without a mark.

"Congratulations," Hasley whispered.

They sat along the fire and ate breakfast together. James moved to sit beside her while Maroon and Amic talked on the other side.

"You should sit with your pair," Hasley said, wanting to support her friend despite feeling sad. The sweater Amic had brought her was warm and she liked the deep green tone. The longer arms helped her feel safe, she tucked into them as she crossed her arms.

"I wanted to check in on you," he said. "I know this must be hard for you."

"You should be happy with your pair. It's your first full day together. That's a big deal and I'm a distraction from that." Hasley tucked back a strand of her hair. It was longer than she had ever had it and more unruly without the hygiene products she was used too.

"You are a welcome distraction, Hasley. I could use my friend right now. Can we talk?" James pleaded, ringing his hands and bouncing one of his knees a few times before he realized and stopped.

Hasley untucked her arms, realizing her selfishness and naivety. She would be there for James. It was okay to feel down given all she was experiencing, but now more than ever she needed to feel connected to those that cared for her. After all, she cared for them too.

"Of course, I'm sorry. Tell me about what is on your mind. What is it like to have a pair?" Hasley asked. Her hand twitched for her pen, wanting to talk to her own pair, but she forced herself not too for his sake.

He smiled hesitantly. "It's really nice to have someone to talk to. We are interested in different things, yet we want to know about our opposing passions. It's nice to know I'll always have that companionship. But," he hesitated to continue.

"What is it?" Hasley prodded. She absently took the breakfast plate Amic handed to her.

"He didn't have visions or dreams like me or hear voices like you. He was where he had to be, just waiting for me. I had to be driven to find him. It reminded me of some fears I had when I was younger," he took a deep breath before continuing.

"I've always cared more about the emotional

connection over the physical. I just don't feel driven by touch. Maroon feels the same. We'll be best friends, spending our lives together. I used to worry about that, since many people seem to look forward to the physical side of a relationship and I wondered if my pair would too. When I started getting those visions and realized I was fateless, that's when the fears came back. I wondered, what if there was no one that complimented me and that's why I wasn't well?" His voice broke on the last word.

"And you were wrong, James. You found your pair. The right person was waiting for you too," Hasley assured him.

"I know. I know that now," James said as a tear trailed down his cheek. He brushed them away. "I am okay now. I have Maroon and I will no longer have those dreams. But why did it have to be me? Why did the gods do that to me? On one hand, I'm so glad Maroon didn't have to experience that. But on the other, I see what you are going through and what you've told me about Arsenio's experience and I wonder. Why not Maroon too?"

James looked down at his feet and whispered, "it makes me feel like a horrible person for even thinking that we should have shared that pain too."

"No, you are not a horrible person. Don't think

that about yourself. You just want to be understood. And as for why it happened to you and not him? We can't know the answer to that. What we can count on is that there is a lesson in this, somehow. We'll find it together if you want, okay?"

He nodded, his whole body shaking. He took a deep breath and let it loose.

"Can I tell you a secret?" Hasley said, hoping to console him. James agreed.

"I feel angry too, at the Gods. But I know that in the end, what I think of Aaleia and Mutrien doesn't matter. What matters is what actions I take with what I have. We have to focus on ourselves and not any other outside influence. We are truly all we have and all we can interact with. When we do that, I know the world will fall into place."

"You really think that, even with how you are living and the pain you feel?" he asked her, eyes crinkling as he surveyed where they were and the wraith asleep on the dirt beside them.

"The alternative is that I can't influence anything. That is unthinkable, so I reject it." Hasley knew that some days that belief was harder to keep than others. There were times where with her condition, all she could do was sit and think of her pain and blame others for it. But when she could, she chose another path.

"Thank you Hasley, that helped. Truly," he said, smiling genuinely at her.

When she bid goodbye to James, Maroon, and Amic, Hasley stopped to write a letter.

> *A,*
>
> *I want to know more about the kingdom you came from, Faeinto. We don't discuss the other kingdoms here. I'm sure they once did, and maybe the older generations that remember free trade still do, but it is a mystery to me and not taught in school. How did the First Fating come together in Faeinto?*
>
> *Here is the story of Ashkadance.*
>
> *Kariana, our first Queen, was the daughter of Zander General. He was in charge of the army that fought against the opposing two continents. She was bred in war, part of the old world before the First Fating. As surely as we are unable to escape our births, she was unable to escape a life in bloodshed and chaos.*
>
> *She fought the dragons with her father, until one day she found love with one. Kariana stood on*

the top of Mount Pietan as Drakul swooped down to meet her. We do not know whether his claws were ready to kidnap the general's daughter or poised to kill her, but once their eyes locked his original intent did not matter. They became fated on the spot. He landed beside her and she dropped her sword. Outstretched she reached for him, but as her fingers dusted his skin he morphed from dragon to man.

I always thought of that as a very romantic scene. We have a statue to commemorate the event and I visit it frequently. I wonder what their first kiss was like, as Drakul had to learn how to be a human at the same time.

I wonder what our first kiss will be like.

Okay, I'm going to change subjects now. Your father was here, he has news. Ember agreed to help, just like I expected her too. And James has a pair. At first I felt jealousy, but I'm okay. I'm happy for him and can't wait to get to know his other half. To bring up kissing again, James said that wasn't what their relationship is like. I do want that though, with us. Assuming you do too. What do you think?

Did you have any friends like that? Who did you spend time with before all of this?

Forever,

Hasley

Hasley,

I like you calling me A. I'm sure it was done in a rush to speak to me and then get my own letter in return, but I still like it. Even if it was for efficiency.

I'm glad you aren't jealous of James. He is now complete, better than before or on the way to it. You can't see it yet, but you are better than before too. You were focused on a perfect life. What do you think of those ideas now? Is it still important to you?

We'll have our own kind of perfect. I can't wait to see who I become at the end of this.

If we had a normal fating, maybe it would have taken you longer to separate from the perfectionist part of you.

I am logical, but in my own way. Just like we all have our own version of perfect, we have our own version of what is logical or realistic. I like to see the world as a game. A game where we all win. Sometimes to win, you have to first lose.

So keep being an adorable loser. Don't worry, you aren't a loser on your own. I'm losing too. But when we meet? That will be a win we will never let down, because our win will help the world. How many people can say that?

And to answer your first question—I plan to kiss you, if you'll permit me. We'll work on the rest of the romantic parts and conversations when we meet.

There are a lot of men and women like James where I am from. Maybe it's the unicorn influence? They don't have sex often as a species. I'm curious how our ruling beasts influence our kingdoms. I don't know. I just realized we haven't spoken much about the fateless. I knew what you meant when you described your symptoms to me, but that's not what we call them on Faeinto and Grydagia. Since we were separate from you, I guess you created your own vocabulary outside of us.

It's not too different though, as we also noted they don't have a fated pair. Our fateless population is called the Pairless. Their names work either way, right? We have wings in our hospital dedicated to them, with volunteers helping to care for them.

My best friend though, my own version of Ember I guess, is named Niandra. She is another trader. Traders don't have many friends that aren't traders or people we trade with. We don't make many connections outside of that.

And as for my kingdom's First Fating, it was quite romantic as well. I'll save their story for when we are together.

I can't wait to talk to you in person, with no delays like this. There is so much I want to know, but only so long I can write without getting a hand cramp.

Yours,

A

SEVENTEEN

BROKEN AND IN LOVE

In no time at all, the carefully transported and packaged dragon blood was sent to the other resistors. Not that Hasley saw any of that, but James and Maroon gave her updates as the days passed. She still hadn't left the forest. She was like an animal, dirty, cleaning herself with cloth and little buckets of water brought by Amic. She didn't have any visitors now but the three of them. Enough support had been drummed up before Ember's appearance, so Hasley gladly took her privacy back.

Maroon brought a brush on one of his visits and helped her comb her hair. He didn't know anything else to do with it, but he brought a ribbon from his sister to tie it up in the back. She grew to like Maroon, even though she envied the companionship between him and James. The nights were a little colder now. They brought clothes and blankets to swap out too. Hasley changed into pants and a long shirt. Both items drowned her, but it was comfortable, and Amic said he'd have her other clothes cleaned.

She was close to meeting him, her pair, and it frightened her. Hasley knew that he was already her pair, but having it officially snap into place as it should scared her. What if he decided he didn't like her and the fating had been wrong? What if something happened to him before then? Hasley and Amic had already told him to stay away from the wall that night, but she still worried.

Hasley pet Amalthea and sent her on her way, a new letter and a new dawn.

"It's today," Amic said as he walked into the camp. She knew that she, Amic, and a handful of people would change the world today. It was always that way, wasn't it? A few people, a cause, and love. She took a deep breath.

He sat on one of the logs they drew around the fire, right outside where her canopy had been. It was like a makeshift living room, this strange pile of dirt near the wall that she lived on. She had awoken early to remove that canopy. After tonight, she wouldn't need it anymore.

Amic ate porridge by the fire in silence. Hasley's voice was sore, afraid to say her fears aloud, but she forced herself to do so.

"What if I'm too broken..." her voice croaked, "for him to love me?"

Amic's eyes swam with tears, putting down his bowl and spoon.

"I've wondered the same thing. Arsenio lived his whole life with his mother, a life without me. Do I fit into it?"

He shook his head and pushed up from the log. Amic walked around the fire and sat beside her. She mutely handed him a corner of her blanket.

"We'll meet him together. We'll be together a lot I think. Whether you and him leave Ashkadance or settle here, I'll come too. I've been alone for too long now, with my pair gone. I want to spend every moment I can with the son that the wall took from me for so long."

He smiled at her and added, "despite our fears, we are not too broken to love."

Tears shed from her eyes and a laugh shook from her. "I used to think that about everyone, but myself. It's time I give myself that same respect, I think."

"Good plan," he said, "now before this show gets on the road, there is one thing we should do."

"And what's that?" she asked curiously.

"We should tell your parents that you are okay. With all that will happen tonight, they should know that," Amic said, thinking of the years he knew nothing about his son's well being.

After a moment's hesitation, she nodded and took out a piece from her large stock of paper.

> *Mom, Dad,*
>
> *I don't know how to start this letter other than to say that I am okay. I have been fated and I hope to introduce him to you soon. I'm sorry for the way that I left and I'm sorry for the pain I caused you both. I love you and will see you soon.*
>
> *I have one request. Stay home tonight, okay? You will know why soon, but for now I need you to trust me when I say that it will be unsafe to celebrate Mutrien's festival outdoors today.*
>
> *All my love,*
> *Hasley*

Hasley savored the last few moments she had of

her old life. While so much had changed in the past few weeks, she knew there were still small pieces of her ready to shed away. She was nervous, but hopeful, to let it all go.

EIGHTEEN

SAVING EACH OTHER

The ground beneath Hasley shook as a dozen other spots along the kingdom's wall were hit with blood fire. Amic pulled her back from the wall for her safety. She struggled at first, but then relented. He held a torch in his hand, lighting his face. His eyes were wide, hopeful, as he stared into its heat. James and Maroon stood behind them, sweaty and leaning on their shovels. Only a few feet from where Hasley usually slept was a fine crack in the wall, one they hoped to split open.

"It's time," Amic whispered.

Hasley felt the outline of Lane's letter in her pocket. Arsenio and her would get to open it soon enough. She smiled at Amic and whispered back, "I'm ready."

"I don't know if I am," he confessed in the dark, taking a shaky breath.

"It's okay to be scared," she said in reply, "but this is where we are meant to be."

He took another deep breath and nodded. "Get behind me."

She repositioned herself behind him and he threw the torch. The fire arched as it landed in the trench they filled with dragon blood. It swallowed up the fire hungrily, boiling up into a rising column of blood fire. Around her the booms of other resistors doing the same along the wall echoed. Other resistors who were hungry for change, willing to risk anything with their own torches fueled by dragon's blood.

Hasley hadn't had the same motivations. A few months ago she would never have done something as dangerous as this, but maybe that's why she needed to. There was so much that she hadn't been able to control these past weeks.

With Aaleia guiding her way, that must be one of the reasons why she was fated to Arsenio, so that she could break that mold. Her and Arsenio needed to be fated for the wall to fall. It was a responsibility larger than she had ever imagined for her life. She was a jeweler. She had wanted nothing but a calm life with a clear path. It seemed so far away from her now.

As the wall that surrounded her for her whole life crumbled down, Hasley held her breath. Her heartbeat quickened and her life started again renewed. Piece by piece, rock and debris fell around them with each boom of blood fire. James and Maroon pulled Amic and Hasley farther back away from the explosion.

When the dust began to clear in the wake of the wall, her and Amic walked cautiously forward. Over the piles of glittering white stone they spotted the strip of land connecting them to the sea. The boat that brought Arsenio to them was tied to a decaying dock, just like she envisioned. The way between them and the sea was full of sharp rocks and still smoldering blood fire, but that did not stop them.

"Let's give them some privacy," Maroon said to James. He nodded in agreement and they watched their two friends disappear. They sat on the log they often had dinner on with Hasley and waited for them to return.

"Arsenio!" Amic called into the dark.

Light from the moon and still burning blood fires lit their way dimly, reflecting back from the water. Hasley was amazed, the ocean was more dazzling than even her visions saw. Such a huge body of water startled her, sending her senses into overdrive.

"Arsenio!" Amic called again. They ran a few feet together on the sand. Hasley almost tripped, unused to the way sand felt beneath her feet.

"I'm here," a voice called to their right.

Hasley turned and was immediately overcome with emotion. Arsenio locked his grey eyes with hers from ten feet away. The gold sparks of their fating finally came together. It latched onto their skin and the space between them began to glow. They ran into each other's arms so swiftly it looked as if the sparks that trailed behind them were wings. Magnetized, their lips locked in passion. The golden sparks between them bounced and expanded until they were surrounded.

"Finally," he whispered against her lips. Her small nose bumped against his wider one and they laughed.

"Finally," she mirrored and moved her face back to see him fully.

His hair was long enough to reach his shoulders, black, and flopping in waves from the sea salt. It was partially contained in a ponytail. His eyes were shining with mischief as he took in her blue hair. His skin stood out brightly in the dark for how light it was, similar to the shine of the moon. He stared at her as intently as she did to him.

"What are you thinking?" Hasley asked him,

worried she wasn't what he expected after all this time. Her old perfectionistic habits momentarily filtered back to the surface, something she would always need to fight.

"You're even more perfect than I imagined, soot on your face and all," Arsenio said as he wiped a finger over the offending spot. She flushed, but smiled.

"I'm glad we didn't describe ourselves. I'm glad I get to have this moment, seeing you as if we were strangers."

His hand caressed her cheek and she basked in the warmth of their true fating. They were whole, together at last.

"My hero," Arsenio called her before dipping down for another kiss.

When he pulled away, they heard a distant voice. His voice grew louder and when she looked, Hasley saw Amic was only a few feet away holding his torch stock-still in the moonlight. She had forgotten she was with him only moments ago. His voice had seemed so far, as if it couldn't filter through their golden sparks. When her eyes refocused, she could see more into the night around her as the sparks bounced high around them. Amic inched closer.

"Son?" he asked.

Arsenio turned his eyes away from Hasley and

saw his father. His eyes seemed to glaze over when he saw his father and a subtler purple light mixed with the gold. Amic and Arsenio had never met, as separated from each other as Hasley had been. This was their blessing bond snapping into place, a father and son reunited at last.

"I'm happy to finally meet you," Arsenio whispered. Amic came towards them and the three of them hugged each other tightly.

In that moment Hasley could see their whole lives stretched out before them in one sweeping wave. This new world would be messy, birthed by blood fire, but they could handle it together.

Because together, their love glowed in the dark of night.

Did you enjoy *Hasley Fateless*?

Leave a review of *Hasley Fateless* and then continue reading in *Kariana Dragon Queen*.

THE
FATED TALES

KARIANA
DRAGON
QUEEN

THREE PRINCESSES.
TWO FORBIDDEN LOVE STORIES.
ONE ULTIMATE BETRAYAL.

R. K. SAMPSON

ALSO BY R. K. SAMPSON

The Fated Tales Series:

Ember Dragon Daughter

Hasley Fateless

Kariana Dragon Daughter

ABOUT THE AUTHOR

R. K. Sampson is a YA and NA fantasy author. Her favorite scenes to write are plot twists, betrayals, and unique takes on love in fantasy settings.

She writes novels that help readers take on scenarios that can seem insurmountable like swift change, massive responsibility, and being different through the backdrop of magic, creatures, and flawed characters.

Rebecca is a mom and married to her high school sweetheart, living in Miami, Fl. You can read her blog chronicling her life and interests on rebeccaksampson.com

instagram.com/fictionbyrks

tiktok.com/@rksampson